The Secret Lives of the Pink House Cats
Prose Poems by Five Felines

D. R. Ransdell

I0553084

Hodophile Books
Copyright © 2025 by D.R. Ransdell
Author Photo by Carol Ekstrom
Additional Photos by D.R. Ransdell

HODOPHILE
BOOKS

Also by D.R. Ransdell

Right Turn to Tucson

Watch for more at www.dr-ransdell.com.

With love to Auntie Carol, without whom there would be no Pink House Cats

Contents

Passing
Night Love
Never Alone
The Last Selfish Act
The Most Precious Gift

4) Ping

Morning Glory
Training Mama
The Professionals
Perfection
Payback
Conquest
Jungle Cats
Art Work
Houseguest
Zen Cat

5) Mei Mei

The Most Beautiful
Late for Dinner
Playmates
In Praise
Broken Rosebuds
Volleyball
Queen of the Shower Curtain
The Fountain
Pink Safari
Nirvana
Uncaptured Beauty

Bandit

BLACK FAVORITE

Mama tells friends she has five cats,
each more precious than the other,
but at The Pink House,
I've always been the favorite.
Mama loved my brother's fluffy fur,
but she's always preferred me,
first because I'm more clever,
and second because I'm black.

Black black, all black,
dark black, lovely black,
black as a moonless night,
black black black.

Mama's parents back in Illinois
had a pet named Dunkelheit,
but that cat wasn't true Darkness.
He had a white patch on his chest
and should have been called Macchiato.

I'm blessed with purity.
Every bit of me is black.
Most humans consider me unlucky
and stay off my path. I like that.
It keeps people from bothering me.
But I'm not bad luck for Mama
because she was born in June
on the thirteenth day of the month.
Black Thirteen they might call us,

a perfect pair.

She snatches me up in the afternoons,
staring into my blackness.
When she holds me up to the sunlight
I know what she sees—
the whole spectrum of the rainbow
reflected in my rich, black fur.

ALPHA CAT

I'm so much the Alpha Cat
that I no longer have to prove it.
Mama thinks I don't care.
She sees nonchalance
when I strut around the house.
It's earned, baby.

I bit Cosmo in the ear three times.
He learned.
Phantom I glared at with eyes
that freeze a lizard at three feet
She took the hint.

The kittens learned slowly.
I bit Ping so hard in the tail
that he couldn't poop for a week
without thinking of me.

From Mei Mei, Little Sister,
I had to draw blood.
She thought she could use
her curvy whiskers
to wrap me around her tail
the way she wraps her tongue
around those juicy June bugs.
I'm immune to her stunts.
The second time I clawed her,
she believed it.

No, I do not have to fight
for the best turkey scraps
or the bedtime space beside Mama.
If anyone forgets who I am,
I set the record straight
with a single hiss.

NIGHT ARRIVAL

As a young cat I lived with a man
who got custody of his daughter
unexpectedly. We arrived together,
me, my brother, and the girl,
on a cold night in November
when the man thought it was safe
to turn off his lights and go to sleep.

He was snoring so rhythmically
when the mother of his child
started knocking on the door
that he didn't hear her.
The woman banged
on the unseasoned plywood
again and again and again
until the child began crying,
and the father, despite
little practice being one,
awoke because somewhere
in his unconsciousness
he heard the cry of his flesh.

He ran through the trailer
in his underwear,
gaping in amazement
to see his nuclear family
huddled on the porch
in the middle of the night.
For a moment he stood confused
while the child clung

to its mother's legs,
and Smokey and I strained
to see through the cracks
in the cardboard box
that passed for a cat carrier.

Then the man remembered
he had manners even when
awakened so abruptly.
He invited us inside,
but the woman balked
as a beagle that comes to
an invisible fence.
"She loves the kittens,"
the woman stated.
"You'll have to take them.
And you'll have to take her
because I simply can't cope."
She thrust us into her lover's hands
and nudged the child inside the door.

Before the man could respond,
the woman returned to her car,
retrieving two suitcases so heavy
that she tottered from side to side
as she struggled to carry them.
She set the luggage on the porch
before speeding off into the night
in a Mustang older than she was.

From the safety of the box,
my brother and I wondered

whether to laugh or curse
our change of fate.

NEW HOME

Our first Tucson home
was a second-hand trailer.
All day we raced to and fro,
pouncing over the bed
as we bounded for the kitchen,
crashing into the cupboards
because we had no space
in which to turn around.
We liked our caretaker
for his friendly voice
and regular meal times,
and though he made us sleep
outside, claiming he couldn't
sleep through our racket,
we didn't run away.

Yet our lives were full of peril.
Though only three years old,
the man's daughter was a devil.
The bigger she got,
the worse she misbehaved,
chasing us from every corner
and squeezing out our breath
because she wanted the man's
uninterrupted attention
each second he was awake.
She broke Smokey's whiskers
because they amused her
and would have broken mine
if I hadn't learned to spring high

upon a shelf she couldn't reach
whenever I heard those
awkward steps upon the tile.

The man reprimanded her,
but the miscreant was deaf
to his command.
Instead she grinned
as she chased us,
greedy, selfish varmint.
She had such a wild streak
that the more the man scolded her,
the more she disobeyed.

One afternoon the man bagged us
in a torn, flannel pillowcase
and drove us across town
to a quiet pink house,
the only residence on the block
whose television set didn't boom
with Super Bowl Sunday.

"This might not work,"
said the woman who emerged.
"They might not like it here,
or they might get lost."
The man assured her
he would take us back
if we didn't work out,
but Smokey and I concurred:
it was far better to live
with a woman who had a yard

than with a rascal in a trailer park.
After we circled the house,
pretending to be particular,
we purred our approval,
and the man sped off before
the woman could change her mind.

Our new mother laughed that night
as we inspected the carpet
and jumped on her table.
She only yelled once,
when we scratched at her couch,
and as soon as we stopped,
she picked us up tenderly,
not crushing our ribs,
not bending our whiskers,
but petting our heads
and welcoming us
to our new home.

AWOL

The first time Mama left town
I was indignant. A young cat
back then, I focused on myself.
Our food bowl was as empty
as the double driveway,
and my resentment crescendoed
in waves of dry, desert air.

Smokey swore she would return,
but I closed my mind to it.
"You have extra fat," I said.
"You can fast for a few days
and it won't hurt you any,
but I'm hungry now."
He pleaded with me to stay,
but I paid no attention.
I waltzed out of the yard,
my silly head held high.

Such a lack of faith
carried its price.
The neighborhood felines
did not welcome an extra cat
calling himself to their supper.
Even the toms across the alley,
who were fed in abundance,
snickered when I asked for a bite
and ran me off the property.

I fared better on Eighth Street.
Two sister cats about my age
let me stay in the garden
and share the stale food
they were accustomed to.
When it got too cold at night
they slipped me inside
through a crack in the window,
but their purpose became clear.
They intended to use me
until they realized I was fixed.

They extended their sympathies.
They thought I was kidding
when I said I preferred
not to have the bother
of impulses or offspring,
and they laughed
when I explained that
the only thing wrong
with my human was that
she'd gone away
without leaving my dinners.

When the sisters begged,
I stayed another night.
They fawned attention on me
because they were starved
for fresh conversations,
but by the next morning
I was exhausted from listening
to so much chatter.

Angry and uncertain, again
I struck out on my own.
Without planning it,
I circled back to Ninth Street,
one block from where I'd started.
I decided to pass by The Pink House
and taunt my famished brother
by scoffing at him with superiority,
but Mama's car had returned,
and so had Mama.

Then my folly became apparent,
for though Mama noticed me
outside the kitchen door,
she wasn't sure who I was.
I held my ground, pressing my nose
to the glass until it hurt.

She finally opened the door,
but her caution destroyed my pride.
I couldn't bring myself
to cuddle up to her and purr
to affirm my identity.
She watched me and waited,
neither encouraging nor stopping me
as I sauntered towards the food.

"Why didn't you greet me
as soon as you heard me come in?"
I asked Smokey angrily
when he lumbered in from the den.

He wedged his head into the bowl.
"Your jump to a conclusion
nearly got us orphaned," he snapped.
A morsel caught in my throat,
for I had never heard him cross,
not even when the devil-child
had bent his whiskers.

"Not five minutes after you left,
Auntie Carol came to pet me.
She brought enough food
for at least a dozen cats
and locked me inside the house
so I wouldn't run away.
She even turned on the TV
so I wouldn't feel alone.
When Mama returned,
they spent long hours
marching around the block
and shouting your name
until Mama started crying
that she wasn't sure
she wanted to keep pets
because it was heart-breaking
if they didn't want to stay.
So don't complain to me
if I don't act overjoyed
to see your sorry black face.
Be glad I don't scratch you
for nearly ruining things."

I didn't have a decent reply,

so I bent my head to the bowl
as if I didn't really care,
hoping I would never need
to learn any more lessons.

THE CAT DOOR

I made a pact with my brother
to never let Mama know
we'd learned to use the cat door
installed especially for us.

It was the prank of teenagers.

We took turns fooling her.
Smokey would go first,
standing by the door panting
as if he'd be ever so glad
to use the outdoor litter box
if only Mama would let him out.
After a few moments
of his mournful staring
and a meow for effect,
she'd get up and slide open
the heavy glass door
though our custom portal
was not one foot away.

Five minutes later,
I'd perform the maneuver
with the same mournful stare.
By then she would be seated
at the kitchen table,
feet up, papers spread.
I would pressure her until
she lost all concentration.

Helpless and unloved,
I would stand before the glass
until she felt guilty enough
to rise once more to let me out.

First she would attempt a lesson.
She'd carry me to the Hale exit
and press my nose to its flap.
"You just have to push through,"
she'd tell me. "Then you can
get in and out all by yourself."
I'd pretend that cold vinyl
was painful to my nose
and cower as if tortured.
She would shake her head,
worried I was a half-wit.
Then she would slide open
the heavy glass door,
waiting impatiently
as I leisurely strolled out.

As soon as she settled down,
Smokey and I reversed the process,
coming to the door singly
and scratching the glass to explain
that we wanted nothing better
than to get back inside.

We played the game all summer,
forcing her up and down all evening
until one day she came home early
and caught me outside

when she knew she'd left me in.
How she praised me!
How she hugged me,
belting "bravo!" into my fur!
That night my saddest look
couldn't budge her from the chair.

Smokey kept up the game
for another three months,
reveling in his power
to make her jump up and down
until one sad night she caught him too.
How she laughed into his fur!
How she petted his shaggy tail!
"See there," she told him.
"I knew you were
smart enough to learn."

SMOKEY

When my brother was two,
he was flattened by a truck.
It was an ordinary truck,
not new, not cool, not red,
a rattletrap belonging to the idiot
who lived across the street.
I say idiot because every time
he picked a new girlfriend,
he fought with her.
Three nights of sex,
then a week of fighting
as they screamed at one another
in that closet of a bedroom
and threw their plastic dishware
across the concrete floor.
I saw it all from the window.
On boring nights, even an Alpha Cat
resorts to crass entertainment.

One July night that same idiot kid
jumped in his truck mid-fight
shouting, "Get out of my life, bitch,"
even though he was the one running.
The kid started his damned engine,
and before my witless brother
could wake from his REM sleep,
his side had been crumpled
into a surgeon's delight.

Smokey died six minutes later,

with me licking his face
though he couldn't feel it.
I love my poor dead brother,
but I haven't forgiven him
for that stupid habit
of crawling under tires
and abandoning himself to sleep.

APPRECIATION

I never appreciated Smokey
while he was alive, ignoring him
on a whim and secretly thinking
I was the superior cat, some days
not bothering to play with him
though generally he was nice to me.

Even the night he was murdered
by that errant motorist, I gazed
at the gray mass on the porch step
without realizing the implications.
Over the next days I pretended
that nothing had changed
though Mama embraced me
more often than usual
and cried into my fur.

I strutted about,
the uncontested ruler,
until the truth hit me
as hail on a car roof:
it's lonely being king.
I slinked down the hall,
lamenting lost opportunities
such as the times I could have
chased fake mice with Smokey
instead of going my own way,
and reprimanding myself
for never sympathizing
with his bitter complaints

about that long, hot hair.

Panicked at my depression,
Mama dragged home two kittens.
Traumatized by the pet shelter,
they darted through the house
as if spirits were inside them.
Hide and Seek, we called them,
but they were even too scared
to find solace in one another.
The girl succumbed to coyotes,
and the boy got squashed,
having forgotten that sleeping
under a car hood
is hopelessly suicidal.

Mama tried another pair,
but Merko constantly complained
about the house and the food
until I encouraged him
to run away, and he did,
while Cosmo found a paramour
and stopped spending nights at home.

Then Mama adopted siblings
that were barely weaned,
but having come from a good home,
they scarcely noticed the change.
Before I could growl supremacy,
they rubbed against me, purring
as they called me their "daddy."

I was powerless against
such innocence. Since then,
I've dedicated myself
to their continuing education
in bird chasing and lizard hunting.
I appreciate my new charges
even when they interrupt my sleep
or steal my treats, knowing
our time together is a gift
and that as the older, wiser cat,
it's my job to make sure
we make the most of it.

THE INTRUDER

One Friday night, the tom
from four doors down
thought he could slur insults
and get away with it.
"You neuters are all the same,"
he claimed. "No guts."
Through the glass door
he'd spotted two mounds
of dry cat food
piled as high as treasure
in a dragon's lair
and took a step
towards our private entrance.

His arrogance was louder
than the football announcer
at the nearby stadium.
"Don't test me," I said,
but he pretended not to hear.
Food was not the issue.
If asked properly,
any of us would have shared.

It wouldn't have taken much:
a simple, Sorry to bother you,
but I'm hungry, or even
Would you mind if I had a snack?
Instead this blob of gray and white
with a broken tooth and dusty fur
sneered at me and pushed

his way inside.

He came back out soon enough,
for Cosmo attacked with a battle cry,
chasing him to my raised paws.
And fight we did, all over the yard,
the ruffian still claiming I couldn't harm him
as I tore his skin with my claws.
I scratched his shoulders and gashed his nose,
calling him names that made Mei Mei blush
and Phantom run and hide in the backyard.

My housemates rarely see me in action,
so Cosmo cheered and applauded,
and young Ping took notes,
vowing to help me out the next time
such a visitor came around.

We haven't seen the tom since.
He's probably licking his wounds
as I lounge around licking mine,
smiling that the price of my pride
and the protection of our cat door
is a simple infection underneath
a couple of puncture holes.

MORNING GREETING

Each morning Mama opens her door
so that we can come and greet her.
She dives back under the covers
to wait for the second alarm.
Sensing the thump thump thump
as we pounce on the bed,
she stretches out her arm,
petting us one by one.
Even with her eyes shut,
she knows who we are
and addresses us by name.

She closes her door at night
for self-protection. Otherwise
Mei Mei and Ping would pounce
on her toes at daybreak,
for they're too young to tell time.
Mama must sleep in peace,
but I'm allowed to join her,
on request, for I'm a heavy sleeper
who never disturbs.

I've earned my special status,
for I curl up by Mama's side,
guarding her against the dark
and lulling her with my purr.
Since she never stirs,
I'm assured a sound sleep too.

Other nights I stay with the kittens,
patrolling the living room,
awaiting the swoosh of the door
and the chirps of the alarm clock.
As we enter the bedroom,
the sun streams through the window,
and we bask in the caress
of another carefree day.

CATS ARE FOR POETRY

With apologies to Billy Collins

At a writer's conference,
a famous poet dared claim
that dogs were for poetry
and cats were for prose.
He made the generalization
not because it was gospel
or because he believed it.
He wanted to get a rise
out of a passive audience
poised on his every word.

Mama told us the story afterwards,
how she had stood and complained
that cats were indeed for poetry,
or at least her perfect pentad,
for she has cultured us extensively.

The wise man briefly smiled,
confessing his claim was false.
Dogs aren't for poetry at all.
Though he's fond of the beasts,
he knows they only love books
for the soft leather edges
they chew when he's away,
using the pages they tear out
to clean their filthy teeth.

The man tried to mask his emotion,
but Mama could see his struggle.
The coup de grâce makes him cry.
No matter the home he provides,
he must bribe his beasts with biscuits
before they'll listen to his work.

Cosmo

LUCKY FAVORITE

I may be one of five,
but I know I'm the favorite
because of how she picked me.
High I sat in my cage at the shelter
where I'd been imprisoned,
praying I might survive.

Mama had chosen another,
a friendly black kitten
with shinier fur than mine
who would be too docile
to ever scratch the furniture.
But then the stroke of luck:
the attendant mentioned
that on this glorious day,
kittens were two for one.

Mama whirled around,
her eyes feasting again
on the hopeful orphans.
I perked right up.
When you're on death row,
it's hard not to overreact
if you know there's a chance.
Despite my young age,
I tried to look sophisticated,
and playful and alert,
and all the other things
she might be wanting in a cat,
and since she'd already chosen

one black kitten, I held out hope
that she might choose two.
When she asked to hold me,
I almost peed on her in excitement,
which would have been a lethal mistake.
But I couldn't control my wild hope.
To think I might be free again!

"Try them together," said the man,
plopping us both on the counter.
"We better make this good,"
I told my rival under my breath.
Because he didn't understand
that his own adoption was assured,
he played along, wrestling with me
as a loving sibling who can't bear
to be alone.

Then I coughed.
How I cursed myself, knowing
one cough would lead to another!
I prayed the woman hadn't noticed,
but she had, and the attendant too.
Because they were both staring at me,
I got so nervous that I coughed again.

My luck held strong that day.
Mama adopted me
though she knew I was sick
and might infect her other cats,
which I promptly did.
But she saw something in me

that I hadn't seen in myself,
something that set me apart.
Did she fall in love with
the high-pitched cry of my bravado?
The delicate slant of my eyes?
The fur that grows in my ears
as tufts of weed in a cornfield?

Mama might have chosen
twenty other kittens that day.
Some were younger and fluffier
and some had better lines.
My life was saved by a miracle
I still can't define.

PERFECT GIFT

During our first family meeting,
we concurred that even though we felt
we deserved more wet food,
we loved our mama
and wanted to show appreciation.
Bandit said it would be ill-advised
to spoil her with too many presents,
so we agreed to take turns.
Then we decided it would be too boring
to always bring the same ones.
Instead Bandit gave assignments:
he would trap lizards, Phantom insects,
and Ping and Mei Mei would tag-team birds.

Bandit consoled me when I complained
that left nothing special for me to give,
nothing that bore my signature.
"Be bold," he told me,
"for good mothers love everything,
and ours is one of the best."
So I brought in a leaf,
a nice, fat, brown one,
transporting it carefully
so that it wouldn't crumble
as I pushed through the cat door.

Mama didn't acknowledge my efforts.
For days she walked by the leaf
without taking a second glance,
and when she did pick it up,

she didn't do so carefully.
My gift broke into pieces
that Mama threw away.

I tried again, this time
bringing in chemistry notes
a student had lost on his way
home from the university,
but my teeth sank through
the formula for iodine,
the ink bled into a blur,
and the paper clumped together
into a useless mound of pulp
that I hid under the refrigerator.

The next time it was my turn,
I chose a candy wrapper,
chocolate brown,
with dainty white letters
and a hint of green.
Mama didn't love this gift either.
She threw my wrapper away
without examining its beauty,
scolding me when I knocked over
the waste basket to dig it out again.

For days I moped around the house,
hinting at Mama's injustices,
but she assumed I was hungry
and gave me extra snacks.
While the kittens presented a sparrow,
Phantom a pair of June bugs,

and Bandit a horned toad
that took him three days to catch,
I had nothing to give.
One afternoon I chased rainbows,
but whenever I bit into them,
they burst apart, spraying color
all over the backyard.

Guilty over his bad advice,
Bandit offered to help.
He led me to the neighbors' yard,
a playground full of beer cans
and broken utensils
and a baseball cap whose rim
had faded into gray.
Then I saw it, the perfect gift,
and I was mad with joy.

I hesitated, worried I might fail again,
but Bandit's eyes were hot with pleasure.
I knew he'd seen the same thing I had,
a simple creation of deliberation.
Triumphantly I brought my present home
even as paint chipped off all around.
Mama's mouth dropped open
when she saw me bring it in.
"How beautiful!" she exclaimed,
and thanked me,
and pressed me to her heart,
and I knew I had done better
than all the rest.

To this day it's not the dead fowls,
the decaying cricket,
or the lizards' tails
that Mama keeps on her desk
to show off to her guests,
but my unique gift of love—
a perfect metal hinge.

THE CHOSEN ONES

Humans are easy to categorize:
those with cats in their hearts
and those without.
Some cat people are retired, of course.
They no longer keep pets
because they are too worried about
what will happen to us
when they pass on.

Others would have cats
if they weren't battling
rednecked, non-cat spouses
or toddlers who treat us as pillows.
Other cat people have to travel
and can't count on friends
to care for us, for they have
no taste in friends,
while others don't have
houses of their own,
and their landlords are dullards
without imagination.

No matter the circumstances,
cat people are the chosen ones.
Because we fill their hearts,
they attach our pictures
to their refrigerators,
buy mugs with our portraits,
frequent friends with cats,
and salivate over us at pet stores,

longing for the day
a feline of their own
will justify their lives.

PRIDE CONTROL

Non-cat people are scared of us
whether they admit it or not.
Stunned by the power of our legs
and the velocity of our reflexes,
they're perplexed by how much beauty
comes wrapped in a ball of fur.
Such people make excuses
that they're allergic to dander
or got scratched once upon a time
so long ago they can't remember
when it happened.

Half of these people
claim that dogs are better.
Canines are merely straightforward.
When they want out,
they pant by the door,
and when the door opens,
they use it.

The other non-cat people
don't like animals at all.
They simply like other things,
such as babies or exercise machines
or toy trains coiling around the room.
There's nothing wrong
with having different taste.
Cats don't even like cat people
in the same amounts.

In fact we should thank heaven
for non-cat people.
If all humans loved us
in dizzying quantities,
our heads would get bigger
than they already are
until they wouldn't fit on our bodies,
and we'd walk around lopsided,
chins bopping on the ground.

THE SLEEP OF CHAMPIONS

We sleep to keep ourselves in perfect condition.
Whether it's the chance to lunge for a moth,
trap a firefly, or attack Mama's toes,
we want to be ready.
We doze most of the time, preparing
for that pristine moment of bliss
when the wayward fowl comes too close.
We capitalize on our opportunity,
giving our prey 120%.
Who says we're not industrious?
We use every ounce of strength
to flex our muscles and gnash our teeth.
Each lizard clenched between our jaws
has the satisfaction of knowing
we've done our best.

Non-cat people assume we're lazy,
ignoring their own eight hours of solid rest,
unscheduled naps, or elaborate excuses
for needing extra sleep. They don't realize
that we snap to consciousness in nanoseconds
without caffeine or snooze buttons.
We never stumble around the house
with the apology of waking up
or need three alarm clocks to arise on time.
All we need is the whiff of excitement
and the hint of challenge
that we sense rather than see.

PRIORITIES

Humans think we run away,
getting lost by accident.
That's not the case.
Instead we try out new homes
in search of a perfect balance
of play and rest.

Even Bandit tried it once
one time when Auntie Carol
forgot to come on time
and the food ran out.
Three places he tried,
each worse than the last
until finally he did get lost.
When he got back home,
he was so happy he vowed
never to roam as far
as the next block.

I thought about searching
for a new place myself,
but Bandit talked sense into me.
"Sure," he said, "spend nights
with your lover. Heaven knows,
nothing will come of it.
But once a day check in at home.
Let Mama know you're around.
If you ever fight with Daisy,
you'll still have a place to go."

I've taken his advice.
Each evening I march in,
meowing loudly
so Mama can't ignore me.
I know what I need:
companions to tease,
scratchable chairs,
pillows in the sun,
frequent petting,
unending food,
roof access.
Such things are important.
All else is detail.

NIGHT IN JAIL

One night Mama put me in prison
without any warning or explanation,
locking me in the spare bedroom
at two in the morning,
right before she went to bed,
preventing my nightly visit
to my paramour.

Mama did not comfort me.
She did not explain.
She left me minimal food and water
and a litter box that smelled like Ping.
Oh, I let her know what I felt.
I howled, thinking she'd made
some horrible mistake
or forgotten what she'd done.
But no, she left me in the bedroom
despite my loudest protests,
and when all the lights went out,
I knew there was no hope.

Locked in the bedroom
as a lion at a zoo,
I remembered the animal shelter
and the ghastly cage I suffered
for two straight weeks
while living on death row.
This time I'd only been a little bad.
I hadn't meant to swipe at Phantom,
but she took me off guard.

I shouldn't have been condemned
just because I drew a little blood.

I couldn't reach the door handle,
but the neighbors' light
shone in through the window,
a beacon of possibility.
I did what any cat would do.
I tried to escape by climbing the blinds.
When they wouldn't hold me,
I bit them instead, braving dust
to gnaw through them
one after the other,
letting the pieces fall to the carpet
as so many casualties.

Mama came for me long after dawn.
I ran for the door, confused.
When she grabbed me up,
I assumed she wanted to hug me
and beg my forgiveness
for the severity of her punishment.
Without so much as a "good kitty,"
she stuffed me into a carrier
and hauled me out to the car.
When the engine monster roared,
I prayed I would die quickly
and not have to suffer.

My eyes were closed so tightly
that I didn't notice
when we stopped moving.

When I dared look,
I was on top of a metal counter
in a room so small
I saw no chance of escape.
A man patted my head
and said "tsk, tsk, tsk"
in a fatherly voice.

"So this is the one
you couldn't catch," he said.
"Three cancelled visits.
I think it's a record."
He picked me up,
and for several long seconds
we stared eye to eye.
I tried to be brave,
but my nose started to run,
and I quivered in his arms.
When he set me on the metal,
I assumed the end was near.
Instead he stroked my fur,
lightly, as if no human
had ever touched me before.
"Don't worry, little buddy,"
he whispered in my ear.
"When will you realize
this is for your own good?"

MAGIC ACT

On the eve of my next visit to the vet,
Mama tricked me into the guest room.
To avoid losing any more blinds,
she squeezed me into a carrier
as if she could really capture me.
Since she thought I'd cry all night,
she shut the door behind her.
A double lock.
I needed three hours to escape.
It was a matter of timing
to lift the latch from the inside
while pushing on the door.

I would have attacked the window
and bitten through the new blinds,
but when I lay down for a nap,
I fell asleep.
I dreamed I'd stuffed Mama
into the closet and locked the door.
How I giggled!
I rolled over and went back to sleep.
In my new dream,
the Cat Council reprimanded me
for imprisoning my owner,
and I had to swear
on a stack of canned wet food
that I didn't know the door would lock.

But oh, the joy of magic!
Mama came for me the next morning,

expecting to find me in the cage.
Instead I was outside it, sniffing, proud.
"How did you do it? How did you do it?"
she muttered as if I would tell her.
She knelt on the floor,
examining the carrier over and over
to see how I'd managed the feat.
I expected a scolding,
which I would have scoffed at,
but instead Mama hugged me,
telling me how smart I was,
how very clever,
and kissing my head
and repeating the praise,
which is why I let her
shove me back into the cage
and whisk me off to the vet's
without performing
any more tricks.

AFFIRMATIONS

Our auntie, who lives down the street,
sings to her cats. They're not sure why.
Singing is not listed in any of the books
for interpreting human behavior.
She sings to them in the morning
while puttering around the house.
She composes each song line by line
to hits she's learned from the radio,
repeating the words over and over
to memorize her creation.
But the subject matter is not
the usual human fare of love
and regret and loneliness.
Her songs are affirmations
she composes for her cats.

They say it started one night
after a so-called friend stated
the obvious: "Ollie sure is a fat cat."
He announced this for no apparent reason,
and Ollie herself agreed that it was true.
The next day Auntie rose early
to start composing.
"You are fluffy beautiful," she began
as if she couldn't feel Ollie's blubber
and instead let herself believe
all that fat was really fur.

Within six weeks all the cats
had their own affirmations.

"Chomsky, I love you anyway,"
began the second song,
composed after Chomsky growled
so vehemently that the cowardly
cat-sitter refused to return.
Then came a country tune for Roz:
"It really doesn't hurt me when you bite."
Auntie crooned that one for a week
as she put antiseptic on her wounds.
Her youngest cat, Wu, received a ballad
explaining why he was born without a tail
while Howard, the clan's spiritual leader,
was awarded a Tibetan chant
consisting mostly of his name.

Auntie sings these tunes
over and over, devising new ones
to highlight additional qualities
she discovers in her cats.
They admit that the songs
are charming in their own way
if you like broken records
or have a dizzy need for affirmations,
but most likely it's therapy gone wrong,
an overdose of optimism, because Ollie,
though lovely, is still fat, and Roz,
though the reigning monarch,
shouldn't be allowed to bite.
But we all have our defects,
and instead of lamenting them,
perhaps it's just as well
our auntie celebrates them in song.

BEAR TRAP

When I sleep, I dream of chasing
black bears on Mt. Lemmon.
I hitch a ride up to the mountain
in the late afternoon
and spend a night camping
to get the feel of the terrain.
In the morning I catch them
stealing into campsites
and clawing through picnic bags.
Imagine their surprise when,
just as they've gotten their noses
into jars of canned delights,
I jump on their backs
and wrestle them to the ground.

They try to bite me,
but I'm too fast for them.
I pounce on their wide necks
and rip their fur with my teeth,
hopping off and teasing them
by crawling into places
they can never reach.
They paw at me, but their wits
are no match for mine.
They don't understand
that the harder they try,
the more they wear out,
for they're strangely lethargic
despite all those months of rest.

After a few simple bouts
of dancing on the beasts
and spitting out clumps of fur,
they realize they're beaten
and ask for my terms.

Victorious, I laugh and run along.

Phantom

MY FAVORITE HUMAN

I prefer the woman not because
she greets me each morning
or fills our bowls to the top
(though I admit that's a plus)
or because her roof is accessible
or her mesquite trees have branches
strong enough to hold me.
I favor the woman because
she's almost never home.

She disappears for hours,
coming home too bushed
to monitor our activities.
The others get jealous
when she stays away.
They don't realize that
the less she knows about
our routines and pleasures,
the less she knows what to expect.
Thus we're unhampered
by human expectations
of when we should eat
or sleep or how much
we ought to purr.

My housemates complain
because they're too immature
to see how sweet they've got it.
I don't tell them otherwise.
If they become disillusioned enough,

they'll run away, in which case
The Pink House and its woman
will be all mine.

PINK HOUSE CAT

I did not set out to be a Pink House Cat.
Like most things, it happened by accident.
At first I resisted. A pink house? For a cat?
But the others seemed happy enough.
High they sat on the slanted roof
overlooking the neighborhood as if
everything that happened within it
was governed by their will.

For two days I circled the house,
roaming up and down the block.
Should I risk it or not?
But I had to make a change.
My owner had moved away
without bothering to warn me,
much less take me along.
I was cold and hungry,
so I swallowed my pride
long enough to give it a try.

I won't call my new home perfection.
Messy from neglect, the residence
is too hot from April through October
(the owner being insensitive to heat),
the TV volume too loud,
the neighbors' mutts too noisy,
and the violin playing too out of tune,
but the water is clean and filtered,
the vacuum cleaner is seldom run,
the cat door opens with a simple push,

and the rooms are full of soft places
where I can shed my fur as I rest.

Except for the few occasions
when the woman dines with guests,
she allows us access to her table
and doesn't bother to yell
if we jump up on the sink.
There are only two rules:
no hissing at other cats
and no scratching the furniture.
We break the rules consistently,
but even if she catches us,
we still get wet food.

I've made up my mind:
I might as well stay.

DAYTIME PLEASURE

What I love the most is a silent room
that you can enjoy all to yourself,
a room so quiet you can hear
the wind whistle, the school bell chime,
or the bus rattle three blocks away.

Your room protects you from
the Doberman two doors down,
the neighbor's SUV, and even
the boisterous nonsense of housemates
who waste nearly all their time
chasing one another.

You sit, comfortable on the bed
in the valley of your own making,
secure in the knowledge that
since the woman has left for the day,
no one will bother you.

You crane your neck, perfecting
your favorite daylight position
because you have no other goal;
everything you want is already yours.

PASSING

They think I'm upset that they ostracize me
and that I dash into the house from fear.
Sometimes they chase me into the back room
as if they were tough enough to terrorize me.

I play along, hissing and hiding under the bed.
Cosmo approaches me the way he does a lizard,
unsure which direction I'm apt to dart.
When I snarl back, he runs away, afraid.

Ping is bolder. He'll raise his paw at me
until we're both hissing, poised to fight.
Then the woman rushes in, panicked,
with the futile plea of any mediator:
"No fighting, no fighting!"

If they knew the battles inside me,
they wouldn't dare come near.
They have scant idea as to my suffering.
Only Bandit has an inkling of the danger
of being on your last ounce of energy
and locked out in the cold.

It happened to him once long ago
when he was foolish enough to think
the catnip was sweeter somewhere else.
When he first saw me, a kitchen stowaway
that frigid February night, he didn't
start a brawl. Of course he might have.

We both knew I'd invaded his territory.
Instead he sniffed at me once to announce
he was boss and sauntered down the hall.

That's how we tricked the woman.
When she first spotted me
grazing at the food bowls,
she chased me out, unsure.
She didn't know I'd heard the news,
that two of her other black cats,
dissatisfied whiners, had run away,
and even though they were both male,
I could slip in through the cat door
posing as either of them.

When she caught me in her house
the second time, doubt filled her eyes.
She didn't chase me away,
for she was an enemy of the cold,
worried I could be one of her own,
and confused by her beloved Alpha,
who hadn't bothered to complain.

So began my best charade.
A few short weeks, I told myself,
until that silly woman catches on
and the nights finally grow warmer,
I'll pretend to be one of those other cats
rash enough to run from a good home,
and I can have free food 24/7
without having to scrounge for it.

What a fright when she imprisoned me
in a carrier and carted me off to the vet!
Sheepishly she told the man that
I was either A5889 or PS4478.
He passed the wand over me repeatedly,
unwilling to believe the obvious:
I didn't have a microchip at all.
I looked to the woman and pleaded
with my biggest, roundest eyes.
Even if she turned me out on my own,
if she paid for all my shots,
I'd have a chance to survive.

It was the vet who saved the day.
"She never was your cat," he said,
"but she knows you're special.
She chose you, not the other way around,
and with cats that means something."
The woman laughed, accepting
his gentle sense of the world,
not because he was older and wiser
but because he was exactly her age,
and she'd always liked the looks of him.

Between Bandit's nonchalance
and the kind doctor's reassurance,
I secured my spot as a Pink House Cat,
and if the young siblings are rude to me,
I don't care. I don't need them
to lick my face or sleep on my shoulder
the way I don't need the softest cushion
or my own can of chunky chicken bits.

My priorities are practical: shelter
from the rain, fresh water, food.

When I really feel like it,
some days I even purr.

NIGHT LOVE

I do not allow petting.
I'm not that kind of cat.
I was so badly treated
as a kitten that I can't
shake the feeling,
even though I know better,
that the woman's touch
could turn into a vicious
beating. Such things happen
to cats and other animals
dependent on humans
for their livelihood.

Perhaps it's only fair.
You could say we're a burden.
Heaven knows we never work,
and the comfort we offer
might not be worth the cost
of collars and vaccines.
The woman is foolish
to have any of us,
but since she does,
I let her know I care.

It's not easy, though.
Too much trust would
make me vulnerable.
So I do not allow her
to stoop and pet me.
Though she's short,

her height gives her
too much of an edge.

Instead I wait patiently
until even that night owl
decides she's had enough.
I listen as she fiddles
with her alarms,
rearranges her covers,
and tilts the blinds.
When she finally
turns off the light,
I wait for silence.
Only then is it time.

I make sure the coast is clear
of all others save perhaps Bandit
before jumping on the bed.
I paw around, verifying
that the woman is nearly asleep.
I pick the softest spot
next to the curve of her legs
or the small of her back,
and then I settle in.

Some nights, a single hand
emerges from beneath
the covers and caresses me.

This, I allow.

Most nights, she doesn't
know I'm there.
Once the writhing stops,
there is no movement at all,
no hand that stretches out
to accidentally startle me
or stroke my silky fur.

On such wondrous nights
I relax into that lifeless form,
soak up slender lunar rays,
and enjoy the woman
the way all humans
should be enjoyed:
in perfect peace.

NEVER ALONE

The other cats think it's strange
that I prefer to be alone.
They assume it's a sign I'm antisocial,
which is true, or that I'm lonely,
which is not.
I'm merely more inquisitive.
It takes hours of concentration
to understand the moon's rays,
the sun's beams, the wind's flow,
a human's moods, a lizard's gait,
or even one another's idiosyncrasies.

I think about why Bandit rolls in the dirt
(his way to feel young),
Cosmo picks fights without provocation
(he would like, some day, to be Alpha),
Ping out-eats everyone at every meal
(once as a kitten he went hungry),
or Mei Mei thinks she's so beautiful
(no good reason).

I invest most hours in analyzing myself:
why I love the feeling of sun upon my fur
(the warmth protects me),
why I prefer to sleep on a slant
(in case I need to rise quickly and hide),
why I'm too lazy to lick my paws
(they get dirty as soon as I go back outside),
or why I prefer June bugs to grasshoppers
(they make a noisier crunch

when I crush them in my jaws).

I'm never alone because
my thoughts accompany me.
Each day poses new questions
I don't have answers to
while each morning presents
a charming new goal—
the chance to contemplate
another piece of my world.

THE LAST SELFISH ACT

The first time the woman took me to the vet,
she had to scare me out of the house
while her friend who lives down the street
stood on the other side of the cat door
waiting to bag me. Not sensing the trap,
I shot into the cat carrier with such force
that I had a headache the whole next week.

A year later, I sensed the danger
the night before when the woman
looked at me with sad eyes
and studied my bedroom,
calculating the most strategic way
to trick me out of my hideouts.

So I was prepared. Before I slept,
I stole into the recesses of the mattress
that I and the other cats
had taken turns shredding into caves.

I awoke before dawn,
listening for the woman's steps.
She tiptoed into the kitchen
as if not to disturb me,
as if I couldn't sense
something was wrong.

When a car pulled into the drive,
I hooked my claws into the bed frame.

When I heard the whispering,
I knew what was awaiting me,
an assistant holding a cage
on the other side of the cat door
as if I were stupid enough
to fall into the same trap twice.

The woman marched into my room
armed with an ancient Hoover
inherited from her grandmother.
She turned it on full force,
expecting the brute machine
would do its usual job of
scaring me outside.

I gritted my teeth at the blare,
praying it wouldn't last.
One second, ten, twenty,
the horrendous roar continued.
When the ruckus stopped,
I thought I could claim victory.

Instead the woman brought
her helper into the room.
I'd seen the short little man before
and thoroughly disliked him.
He never paid attention to us
though he claimed to be "good with cats."
If the kittens were friendly enough
to jump into his lap, offering friendship,
he shooed them off without hesitation
as if his wrinkled, unwashed jeans

were too clean for us.

Worst of all, the woman was always
sadder after he left than before he came.
I panicked, realizing the man's presence
was my fault. Before I could revise my plan,
the man had dived under the bed for me.
As I drew blood, I realized the woman
would somehow have to pay.

So I went limp, and the man,
congratulating himself on his triumph,
bundled me into the cat carrier.
The woman thanked him,
promising a special "dinner"
as he scurried away.

She told me I was a good cat,
but I knew it was a hideous lie.
My fear had blinded me
into thinking only of myself.
All the way to the vet's,
I choked on my remorse,
vowing to reform.

THE MOST PRECIOUS GIFT

One summer the woman was gone so long
that she asked a friend to help care for us.
He would whiz into the driveway
on his fifteen-speed bicycle,
wiggle off his helmet,
and catch his breath
in the cool of the kitchen
as he dripped sweat on the floor.
He would open a can of tuna
to get our attention, unaware that
as soon as he approached the house,
all our eyes were on him.

He loved us though he didn't know us,
piling the food high enough
to last an entire week
and cleaning the water bowls
instead of merely refilling them
the way other caretakers did.

Bandit and the kittens played into his hands,
falling over themselves as clowns to greet him,
each trying to get more petting than the other,
each pretending to be the favorite cat.

One evening the cyclist came after dark.
Long after the others tired of his attention
and scampered out to play,
he sat on the couch with a notebook,

barely moving his pen across the page.
Then he stopped writing altogether,
his gaze frozen into space.
I was afraid he'd fallen dead,
and we'd have to suffer two weeks
of a corpse fouling the living room.
Finally I realized it was he watching me
instead of the other way around,
watching stealthily so that
I wouldn't get scared and run away.

I had never encountered a human
wise enough to comprehend.
To show my approval,
I leapt to the arm of the couch
and stepped forward close enough
that the man could stretch his hand
far enough to pet me.

As long fingers massaged my neck,
I knew my instincts were right;
this man was special.
He knew pain.
It was his constant companion.
That's why he could keep so still.
He was used to sitting patiently,
forcing out his own sensations.

Though the sting of abandonment
strikes the heart and not the body
and my wound was not fresh,
I shared his torment.

I understood his sleepless nights
and the numbness of being trapped
as he understood why I couldn't
clamor for his attention.
While he scratched my head,
though he couldn't hear it,
I even purred.

When the other cats returned
from their hourly patrols,
anxious to share their exploits,
I slinked away. When I looked back,
the man still smiled. He'd gained
the others' love the easy way
with fresh catnip and extra treats.
From me he'd gained
something far more valuable—
a skeptic's priceless trust.

Ping

![Kitten playing with a string toy]

MORNING GLORY

Mama tries to keep it hidden,
afraid it'll go to my head,
but I know I'm the favorite.
Why wouldn't I be?
I'm the perfect kitten
in glorious gold and white
with a candy cane tail
and a splash on my cheek
to give me panache.

My balance is perfect:
not too much gold,
not too much white,
perfect ying/yang
though clearly I'm a male
without too many feminine traits.

Each morning I rush to greet Mama
as soon as the alarm goes off.
Slowly she slides one hand
from beneath the covers,
braving the morning air
in her hurry to pet me.
I circle her and purr.
When I bite her toes,
she rewards my exuberance
by flinging me off the bed
because she knows how much
I love to soar through the air.

TRAINING MAMA

"I'll be back soon," Mama shouts
as she heads out the door.
She lies because she feels guilty
about leaving us alone.
We act neglected,
but as soon as that bike
glides down the driveway,
The Pink House is ours.
On Fridays we have a treat.
We steal into the bedroom,
jump up on the chair,
and sink our claws into the fabric,
congratulating each other
as the white burlap starts to rip.

She used to spray the chair
with Orange Away,
not guessing it was too old
to irritate our nostrils.
Next she spent hours
applying Kitty Tape
but got so frustrated
peeling the strips apart
that she didn't use enough
to keep us away.

One day, angry to notice
more loose threads,
she booby-trapped the chair
with circles of strapping tape.

Phantom warned us
during another failed bid
for our acceptance.
We took the hint.
Tape with such strength
can clog your nose
or, worst of all,
break a whisker.

We started to whine
about Mama's unfairness,
but Bandit shut us up.
He claimed we were overreacting
because the solution was simple
as long as one of us
was willing to sacrifice
a few tufts of fur.

While Mama prepared her dinner,
we stole to the bedroom.
We helped Mei Mei back herself
into the biggest sticky circle,
directing her as a truck driver
backing into traffic
until the tape snapped to her tail.

As soon as Mama sat down to eat,
Mei Mei raced into the dining room,
thrashing about the furniture
as if the devil pursued her.
She crashed into the table,
spilling Mama's piles of work.

She jumped on and off the desk,
knocking over a jar
of vinyl-coated paperclips
that spread all over the floor
as a row of dominoes.
Then she sprinted into the kitchen
and back out again as if
she'd never ever been so scared.

Mama couldn't catch her.
Back and forth they ran
until Mei Mei collapsed,
panting and writhing
as if she'd die of pain.
Mama cried apologies,
liberating one damaged tuft
of fur at a time.

By bedtime that tape lay in the trash.
We celebrated by singing an ode to Fridays
and playing noisy games of rooftop tag
as soon as Mama turned off the lights.

THE PROFESSIONALS

The first time we went to the vet,
we wailed all the way to the clinic
only to be laughed at by the dog
strolling as a prince on a leash
because he didn't have a cage.

When Dr. M. entered the room,
I hid in the corner so that
I wouldn't have to go first.
When he pulled the gun
on my sister, I shut my eyes,
but Mei Mei didn't notice.
When my turn came,
I barely felt the pricks.
Though I had to sleep it off
for the rest of the day,
I didn't really mind.

The next time we met
a woman with a soft blouse
and a friendly smile
big enough to swallow me.
Her hugs took my breath away,
but when she praised
my white and gold fur
I relaxed in her arms.
She was such an expert
that I never felt the shot.

It wasn't until later that
we understood our fortune.
Neighbor cats told of vets
who saw dollar signs
instead of skin irritations,
performing exams too briefly
to notice signs of trouble
but charging fees all the same
and knocking out the patients
for expensive teeth cleanings
they didn't yet need.
Such imposters hired assistants
that were so laissez-faire
they mixed the animals up,
giving Fluffy a vaccine for Dusty
and Rascal a three-year rabies shot
two years in a row. Those quacks
couldn't be bothered
to groom the difficult cats
or take time to pet them
even though they could see
the fright in their big green eyes.

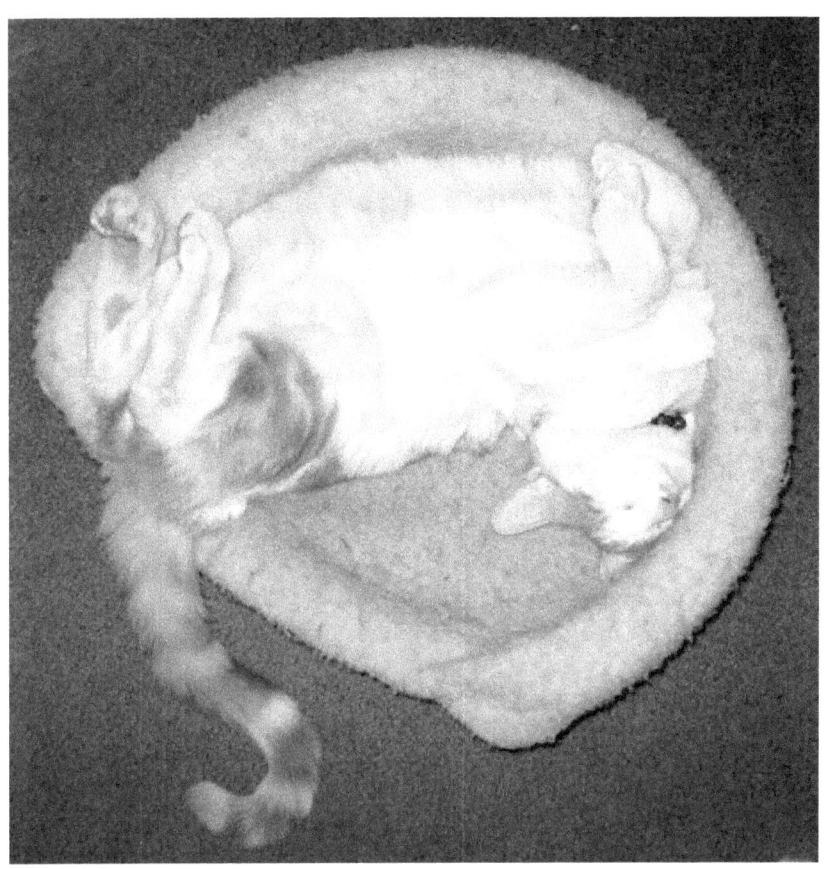

PERFECTION

On lovely days when
the temperature is 82,
the sky shows no storms,
fresh water fills my bowl,
and my belly is full of treats,
I'm too happy to chase lizards
or sparrows or butterflies
or spy on the neighbors
or take lessons from Bandit
or lick Mei Mei's excess fur.

On those perfect days
I find a perch on the roof
or in the palo verde tree
or on top of Mama's car,
and I take in the view.
I reflect on all the things
I have to be thankful for,
such as a sister to chase
and a toy mouse full of catnip,
and by then I'm so sleepy
that I rest my head on my paws,
celebrating my perfect world.

PAYBACK

Mama thinks we don't understand
that she leaves us weekday mornings
because she has to go to work,
but we know that catnip isn't free,
and we do like our luxuries.
We also know that on weekends,
she could spend all her time with us.

Last Saturday she left at dawn
to go hiking in the desert.
When she got back home,
she was too worn out to say hello.
We could have helped her relax,
but then she rushed out
to visit so-called friends
who won't visit The Pink House,
claiming we make them sneeze.

Mama came home a second time,
long after dark, and worse,
hours after our dinnertime.
Even though she opened
a can of beef in oyster sauce,
we gave her the cold shoulder.
She was too drained to notice.
She closed her bedroom door,
shutting us out once again.

After the lights went out,

we waited for the silence
of Mama's deepest sleep.
Then we began our revenge.
I snarled at Mei Mei,
who snarled at Cosmo,
who snarled at Phantom
even though she wasn't there.
"That's enough," Bandit said.
"Wait." And we did, but
Mama made no sound.
"Again," Bandit commanded.
We snarled as loudly
as we could, hamming it up
in our best dramatic roles.

When Mama's light went on,
we scattered, holding
our laughter between our tails.
Mama rushed from her room
to reprimand the culprit,
but since we had retreated
to separate hideouts,
she couldn't figure out
who had started the fight.
She went back to bed,
shifting anxiously since
we'd so successfully
disturbed her peace.

We positioned ourselves
for the next round of attacks.
First we waited for silence.

Then I began with a howl
that came from the depths of
my dirty white belly.
Bandit answered with sneers
I'd never heard before,
and Mei Mei roared a reply.
Cosmo joined in until
we were a chorus of growls
smashing every shadow of peace.

Mama burst into the hall
only to find it empty.
She ran into the living room,
but no one was on the couch
or even at the food bowl.
She checked the guest room,
but we weren't lying on the bed
or sprawled over the burlap chair.
We were hiding in the study,
our muffled giggles
nearly exploding us.

The third time we roused her,
she was furious, yelling
that we were ungrateful
and that we needed to get along
if we expected her to shelter us.
She ran from room to room,
nightie off her shoulder,
hair sticking out, too exhausted
from her hiking and gossiping
to see through our tricks.

After that we let her sleep,
chuckling to ourselves
as we vowed to make
even more racket
the next time she chose
to spend her whole Saturday
far away from us.

CONQUEST

On lazy afternoons
we tiptoe along the fence,
showing off our perfect balance
and proving beyond argument
that while fences discourage dogs,
they're no barrier to cats,
making us the true rulers
of the environment.

Even before I reached puberty
I chased my sister up a mesquite tree,
daring her to go to the highest branch,
hoping she would fall off the limb
so that I could make fun of her.

Instead she darted to the roof.
I'd never jumped so far,
but I had to follow or lose face.
I leapt twenty feet off the ground,
pouncing into unknown territory
despite all possible dangers.

I could not have imagined
such a wondrous scene.
I lost interest in the chase,
for I'd won the neighborhood,
observing backyards
in every direction.
I spotted Mama down the block

chitchatting with Auntie,
Bandit courting the alley cat
who was paying no attention,
and Cosmo chasing Phantom
in the sagebrush next door.

Mei Mei backtracked,
convinced I'd hurt a paw,
but when she reeled around,
she understood. We scampered
between corners of the roof,
thrilled with our new roles
as undisputed masters
of the Pink House world.

JUNGLE CATS

We have two older brothers
that we rarely see,
Kepler and Copernicus.
They're inside cats.
They live with a man
four miles away,
which might as well be
the other side of the world.
We visited one night, but
the journey took three hours,
and the visit several more.
We were so worn out
when we got back that
we had to rest the whole next day,
and our noses were raw
from pressing against the screens.

The man keeps our brothers
in a big house where
they run back and forth
and down the hall all day long
and even into the night.
The man loves them too much
to let them go outside,
for he lives on a busy street
and is a cautious man in every way.

For winter entertainment,
he lies on his back
so they can use his stomach

as a trampoline.
In the spring he brings them
blades of Bermuda grass
so they can pretend
they're in the jungle.
They fight over the slender tufts,
batting them about as enemies.
Then they gobble them down
and throw up on the carpet.

On summer afternoons,
they watch out the window
wondering about the world
and contemplating escape.
One day last year the man
forgot to close the back door.
Kepler poked his face outside,
but the sunlight bit his eyelids,
and the 108-degree air
choked his throat
until he couldn't breathe.

He ducked back inside
and warned his brother not to try it,
but siblings rarely listen.
Copernicus had to try it for himself.
He strolled outside on the sidewalk,
but the cement scalded his paws,
and a passing truck honked
with such an earsplitting noise
that he crashed into the door
in his hurry to get back home again.

When the man came in
from the garage and saw
the open door, he panicked.
His heart boomed in his chest
as speakers at a rock concert.
He cursed himself for his inattention
and phoned his friends
to help in the rescue search.

Just as suddenly his panic ended.
When he caught sight of a gray tail
and a yellow paw, he knew
that both our brothers
were resting safely in the house,
wrapped inside his love.

ART WORK

Here's more proof I'm the favorite:
I get away with everything.
On special nights,
Mama lets me hide in her backpack.
I crawl amongst the papers
even though she knows I might
bend the edges of the books
or scratch the lining of her bag.

Last night I chewed through
a perfectly good folder,
an expensive one, I think,
to judge by its thickness
and the trouble I had
piercing its plastic hide.

When Mama retrieved the folder,
she held it to the light,
studying the tooth marks
planted at irregular intervals.
First she viewed my creation
right side up, and then
she spent just as long
examining it upside down,
deciding which angle was
the most beautiful of all.

She admired my handiwork,
patting me on the head

and calling me a good boy,
acknowledging my efforts
to create a piece of art
made specially for her.

HOUSEGUEST

We saw she was scared by the cautious way
she opened the car door, looking around,
afraid we would pounce, and then Cosmo did,
attacking the ankle that she pulled back into the car
as if she preferred to return to the airport
without visiting Mama at all.

Mama coaxed her friend inside,
assuring her we would behave.
How we snickered!
When it comes to us,
Mama exaggerates the positive.

We waited outdoors until the women were
ensconced in the couch, feet up, shoes off,
too relaxed to be alert,
too keyed up to be together
and deep in their gossip to notice
where we were or what we had planned.

Mei Mei won the draw, performing
a left-side pounce to the couch arm
on which the guest rested her back
before bounding to the middle cushion
and off to the floor.

The woman yelled as she sprang to her feet,
so shocked she might have died of fright.
I laughed so hard I almost peed on the rug,

and even Mama joined in,
apologizing for our behavior
while tears ran down her face.

An hour later, I won the next round.
I performed a straight-up pounce,
and though she saw me coming,
the guest still shrieked
and scrambled to her feet
and halfway around the room.
I would never have guessed
that a human could be more fun
than the stubborn horned toad
we kept trapping in the garden,
but whenever we attacked,
she overreacted in a different way.

We might have continued the game,
forcing the victim to squeal
with our attacks and counterattacks,
but when she looked tired,
Bandit insisted on taking his turn.
Indeed he saved the best for last,
perching himself between the women,
taking a big breath, and pretending
that everything in his stomach
was about to come back out
the same way it went in.

The guest stood and shouted,
upsetting an empty glass
that rolled off to the floor

and a bowl of chips that
scattered every which way.
Mama picked Bandit up
and scooted him outside
so she wouldn't have to launder
the cushions. The second time,
he pretended to vomit on the rug,
but by now Mama understood
his coughing was an act.
She hugged him and winked,
our co-conspirator,
advising her friend to ignore us
while they continued their chats.

The lady stayed for three days,
but she never relaxed at The Pink House.
Each morning she opened her bedroom door
inch by inch so we wouldn't rush in
and investigate her suitcases.
Ever alert to more antics,
she would tiptoe down the hall,
worried we would streak past
in a flash of energy she couldn't control.

Each evening she sat with Mama,
but instead of relaxing,
the guest watched over her shoulder
to make sure we weren't attempting
another surprise.
When she left a few days later,
we were sorry to see her go.
Even though we invited her

to come back soon
by biting her luggage straps
and shedding hair on her ankles,
we haven't seen her since.

ZEN CAT

The day stretches before us
without schedule. I arch
my back in a graceful curve
and reach towards Bandit,
who sits watching me as calmly
as he always does.
Wise and content,
he's the Zen cat,
the master who sits
reflecting on his experiences.

He shares them with us so that
we won't make his mistakes,
such as ignoring his brother
while he was still alive,
jumping onto a roof without
a plan for getting off,
or running away because
dinner was served
a day or two late.

He loves us enough
to share these things.
While I may have gotten stuck
atop the cabinet
and once on the third branch
of the chinaberry tree,
Bandit gave me the courage
to get back down.
Even when Mama yelled at me

three days in a row
for scratching her new couch
and forgot to give us catnip
for a week, I never thought
of running away.

Every day I lick my sister
though she growls at me,
I nap in the rays of the sun,
I meow at Mama to remind her
how important we are,
and I purr at Bandit,
my teacher, master cat.

If I work hard at napping
and relaxing and reflecting,
someday I might become
the Zen cat myself,
expert storyteller and guide,
counselor and coach,
purring for days on end
to celebrate my world.

Mei Mei

THE MOST BEAUTIFUL

I'm so beautiful that
I can hardly stand myself.
Black, beige, and white
in exquisite combination,
the tri-colored wonder.

It wasn't always like this.
When I was small, the man
who lived in my first house
called me Yoda, claiming
I was ugly and assuming
that I wouldn't know
I was being insulted.
Silly man.
Yoda is wisdom.
Ask anybody.

When his wife carted me
and Ping away because she was
tired of our antics, I sneered
because the man was parting
with the most precious possession
in his whole, ordinary house.

He realized it later
when he came to visit
at my new home.
He pretended to laugh
at his mistake, but when

he tried to touch me
I flicked my tail in his face.
You don't insult Mei Mei,
Little Sister,
without paying the price.

I'm not beautiful by accident.
Bandit and Ping think it's natural
I'm so fine. They don't see that
while they're taking extra naps,
lazing away the day, I'm at work
lick, lick, licking all morning
to clean my back and belly
so that I have all afternoon
to lick my paws and tail.

I don't take such measures
out of vanity. It's my duty
to look my best, not for the boys
or to compete with Phantom,
but for my mama, because
she agreed to take me in
even when she expected,
given the man's lame description,
a wrinkled rat with twitchy ears.

When Mama holds me,
she marvels proudly
at the designs on my cheeks,
the swirl of colors
that decorate my back,
the white gloves on my paws,

the sparkle of my radiant belly,
and above all, the lush softness
of my groomed fur.

When I want down,
she lowers me gently
to avoid ruffling my coat.
She bends close to my ears
and whispers, "You're beautiful."
I purr at her and smile,
pretending she's told me
what I don't already know.

LATE FOR DINNER

When Mama ignores me,
I teach her a lesson
by coming home late for dinner.
After summoning us
with clicks of the tin lid,
she divides our portions,
carefully separating
the chunks onto different plates
so that Ping can't gobble up
everybody's share.
When she realizes that
four cats are feasting
but I'm not in sight,
she panics.

Mama can't imagine that
I'm busy testing my balance
on high palo verde branches,
scratching the neighbors' sofa
that sits on the front porch,
stalking the horned toad
that lives in the back yard,
wishing for a hummingbird,
or plotting against the mutts
who bark all day next door.

Mama imagines catastrophes:
she's certain that I've been
flattened by the mail truck
or kidnapped by evil children,

that I've lost my way
by leaving Ninth Street,
or worst of all, because
she hears the snapping
of my smallest bones,
that a coyote ate me up.

She paces inside the house
unable to concentrate.
She looks out each window
before checking places
I may have gotten locked into,
such as the laundry room
or the kitchen cabinet.
Then she peers into the dark,
praying I'll come home
and kicking herself for not
paying me more attention.

After she finally sits down,
exhausted by her imagination,
I give in. I waltz through
the cat door pretending
that I'm right on time.
She swoops me up and
tells me I'm so precious
she couldn't live without me.
I wallow in needless praise,
meowing appropriately.

Better yet, she opens
an extra can of cat food

and gives most of it to me.

PLAYMATES

Under the sink in the kitchen,
Mama keeps a Lizard Rescue Jar.
She thinks we don't know what it's for,
but in fact it's clearly labeled with
a crude drawing in Mama's hand.
We delight in chasing the creatures.
We bring them in through the cat door
to play at leisure in the living room.
When Mama sees us swoosh our tails
as we regard the bottom of the couch,
she knows we've got one.

Then starts the game.
Mama bribes us with treats
so she can rescue the lizard.
She chases it around the house,
tearing down stacks of books
to discover its hidden alcoves,
grabbing its tail, which detaches,
and squealing as she traps it.
The *thunk* of its head in the jar
marks the end of the round.

When she thinks we're unaware,
she releases the prisoner outside,
never understanding that
we were playing hide and seek
and would have returned the toy
to its home among the jade plants
if she'd given us more time.

We win either way.
If the lizard survives the rescue,
we wait until it grows back a tail
and regains its strength.
Then we chase it around the yard,
carry it back through the cat door,
and chase it under the couch
so that Mama can rescue it
all over again.

IN PRAISE

I praise the sun,
its brilliant intensity
beaming rays into my fur
until my back muscles stretch,
my side trembles in warmth,
my paws flex to the sky,
and I open myself
to the world.

I praise the moon,
guide to midnight romps,
accomplice to nightly prowls
and silent, trusted companion
that protects The Pink House
with a silver spotlight.

I praise my cushion,
the softest in the house,
the one earmarked for me,
though I must share it with Bandit
and guard it against my brother,
who scratches the fabric
when I'm not watching,
hoping to gain control.

I praise my exquisite fur,

my inimitable, tricolored fur
that makes me so undeniably lovely
all the other cats I know are jealous.
Even Bandit, for all his blackness,
senses that if it came to a contest,
I would beat him every time.

I praise my lush cat life
of naps and butterflies and petting.
The others claim Ping and I are spoiled
because we've never suffered cat shelters
or depressing homes with empty food bowls.
We compensate with mindless fighting
and hissing and endless chasing
as if something were wrong
with our privileged lives.

BROKEN ROSEBUDS

My special scratching post
awaits me in the living room,
an oasis at the end of the space
between the couch and the wall.
The spot belongs to me alone,
uncontested because the others
are too fat to reach it. Even I,
the daintiest of the house,
have to squeeze in carefully
so I don't get stuck.

I visit my hideout
during afternoon lulls
when the others are asleep
and work on the upholstery.
Gloriously I raise my right paw
to the ragged crater I've made
in the blooming lavender flower.
The fabric is of the finest quality,
so I needed five straight weeks
to claw my way through,
breaking the threads
one at a time.

On alternate days I work
on the other craters instead,
such as the one in the pink rosebud
or the one in the light green stripe,
making a connect-the-dot pattern
of my own unique design.

Such artwork is ecstasy.

Sometimes I can't wait for my daily fix
of artistic beauty and attack the couch
even when Mama is home. I start quietly,
sinking only one nail into the fabric,
and then another, and then finally,
I can't stand the temptation any longer.
I attack full force in a catnip frenzy,
losing my head to the thrill of the kill.
Mama yells as if I were deaf,
stretches a hand into the narrow corridor,
and flushes me out. She transports me
to the cardboard scratching box
as if she were doing me a favor.
I love Mama, so I pretend to scratch
for a moment to appease her,
knowing full well that in a few hours
she'll either be gone or asleep,
and once again I'll have my secret corner,
my personal paradise, all to myself.

VOLLEYBALL

What we live for is a challenge.
Do you think we enjoy
the taste of feathers?
Usually they're full of dust,
but chasing an animal
that carries its escape plan
on the side of its body
is too delicious to pass up.
By logic we shouldn't
ever bring down a bird.
We're highly visible,
and most of the time
we're wearing bells.
No wonder we feel joy
when a winged creature
falls to our clutches!

We rejoice over lizards too
because they're small enough
to slip between cracks of fences
and scurry to the tops of trees,
so really, there's no excuse
for their surrendering to us
unless they're weary of life
and ready to move on.

Live creatures naturally make mistakes.
Our purest challenges are mechanical.
Oh, the pleasure of breaking a ball-point pen
by flinging it from the desk to the floor

a thousand times until it hits just right,
bending the wires of the TV antennae
so the channels never stay in tune,
or, best of all, ruining a doorstop
through constant bouts of volleyball!

After we've chosen our target,
the first days are the most difficult.
The doorstop barely yields to our paws
even though we tag team against it.
It takes days to weaken the coil
enough to get a satisfying sound.
Then we bite off the plastic tip
to lower its morale.

We start a new round of attack,
fifteen games each afternoon
in a regular tournament,
taking bets on the winner
who delivers the final blow.
We play extra rounds,
batting the coil to and fro
in a climax of energy
until the metal gives out,
popping off the wall
in a burst of speed
and lying dead on the rug
as we kick it around.

QUEEN OF THE SHOWER CURTAIN

People who don't have cats
assume we're destructive.
Au contraire.
We perform a vital function
by forcing home improvements.
I've worked hard all week
to defeat an aesthetic foe:
the cheap shower curtain
whose orange and aqua buds
ruin the guest bathroom décor.

Those neon tulips have no place
among the De Grazia children,
the poppy field of Monet,
the blue glass gondola,
the Greek ship arriving into port,
or even the porcelain orchestra
of teddy bear musicians.
All those I can stand.
Even if they don't fit together,
they don't offend my eyes.

But the garish curtain made in China
has nearly driven me from the house.
I don't care if the monstrosity
came from a thankful houseguest.
That plastic garbage is coming down.
Each morning I attack the offender,
weakening its resistance by biting the fringe,
clawing the hooks, victory near.

How I persist! Soon I'll break the rod.
As it plummets from the wall,
I'll dodge the plastic as a soldier,
risking my life for the sake of art.
I'll celebrate as I feast on my war spoils,
ripping the curtain until it's dead
and not resting until it's buried
in the outside rubbish bin.

I'll enjoy the sleep of angels
knowing that thanks to me,
in Mama's Pink House,
beauty reigns.
Only when I've rested
will I decide which enemy,
out of multiple possibilities,
most deserves the top of my list.

THE FOUNTAIN

The liquid dances, putting on a show.
I grasp as it leaps and swooshes,
but it leaps beyond my control,
impatient to disappear down the hole.

How I love to watch it swirl!
I bend my face to its kaleidoscope,
nearly joining the merry-go-round.

The water bowl I share with the others,
who push and shove as I arrive,
but the porcelain oval is mine alone:
fresh, cold water in endless quantities
performing for my pleasure
as Mama leaves the room.

PINK SAFARI

We spend our most treasured evenings
scaring Mama's frequent guests.
Though thirty times our size,
they can't mask the panic
as they come inside.
No! say their eyes.
Do not come near,
for you're dangerous.
We're but weak humans
without sufficient powers
to protect ourselves against
the wild beasts of Mother Nature.

Such fear is our favorite invitation.
We retreat as if we empathize,
hiding around the corner
with the savvy patience
of starving panthers.
Our prey relaxes as
gazelles enjoying shade
or water buffaloes at a waterhole.
Such guests come to relax with Mama,
not suspecting they're the entertainment.

We take turns, my brother and I.
First Ping distracts them,

leaping into the room
as if pursuing
a mountain goat
that must be captured
before it destroys the environment.

While the intruders watch Ping,
terrified of busted teeth
and blood spatter,
I stage my attack,
my sleek body soaring
until I land on the cushion
so hard that I rock the couch.

On good days the guests spill drinks
or let loose their paper plates,
sending a dozen crumbs
over Mama's carpet.
Others leap to their feet,
worried they're risking their lives,
unable to relax for fear of a repeat assault.

The jungle hunters retreat with dignity.
Once again the humans are conquered
by the masters of the living room.
If the outsiders dare return,
they know to be vigilant,
for the Pink House lions,
most valiant of creatures,
always keep up their guard,
never thinking of themselves,
performing their best secret attacks

to protect Mama against her many guests.

NIRVANA

Mama's friend was horrified
when I brought a grasshopper
into the middle of the living room
and proceeded to tear off its legs.
One by one I crunched them
while the guest observed in pain.
"That's disgusting," she cried,
but she didn't look away.
She was fascinated by the way
I ate up each limb as if it were
a stick of smoked barbecue,
licking my whiskers between bites
to make a better show.

Though Mama disapproves
of snacking in the living room,
usually tossing us outside
bird in mouth, she never disturbs us
when we bring in grasshoppers,
preferring that we finish them off
all in one meal.

Mama doesn't favor such insects.
She tells of a zoology class
and a writhing specimen
that should have been dead
given that a pin pierced its torso
but instead kept spinning its legs,
struggling to release itself.

So even though Mama
was watching me,
I knew she didn't mind.

The visitor was aghast, asking
Mama how she could stand
this example of nature's cruelty.
The woman doesn't own pets
but has only one small child,
so she knows little of our ways.
Then again, neither does Mama,
who claims we act on instinct.

We perform a higher function.
Cats, you see, are mostly Buddhist.
We're not simply killing our quarry.
We're helping the victims reach
their own next levels.
Why would any creature
choose to be a grasshopper?
It's not by self-selection.
Their spindly legs
don't fit their bodies,
and their assonant voices
even cause crickets to run away.

Such insects are better off
cycling out of their rotation
and hoping for a higher entity.
Why waste time as an atrocity
when there's a possibility,
no matter how remote,

that you could become a cat?

UNCAPTURED BEAUTY

My beauty is too vast
to fit into a photograph.
No machine can capture
the fluff of my fur
or the glistening of white
against beige or black.
I fit no frame, yet
Mama snaps my picture
at least every other day.

She stalks me
with her latest camera,
imagining that
she can take enough shots
to reproduce me.
She stands no chance.
She can't capture my splendor
all at once no matter
how many times she tries.

The truth is simple:
perfection can't be copied.
I've seen her efforts,
but her blacks are too black,
the beiges too beige,
the whites too off-white.
No mere photo duplicates
the grace of my step
or the attitude I include
in the flick of my tail.

Mama must appreciate me
the natural way, marveling
at my charm and beauty
each time she greets me
and snuggles me in her arms.

Author's Note: I hope you've enjoyed getting to know The Pink House Cats. They've certainly enjoyed the chance to show off! If you enjoyed reading their stories, please leave a review on your favorite social media sites.

D.R. Ransdell resides in Tucson where she can enjoy outdoor swimming all-year round. She writes mysteries about mariachi violinist Andy Veracruz and travel novels about journalism student Gina Campanello. During the school year she teaches writing at the University of Arizona, but she spends summers abroad, often visiting relatives in Italy and Switzerland. Please visit her at http://www.dr-ransdell.com

Hodophile Books strives to entertain readers with humorous fiction and fun stories that take readers around the world. https://hodophilebooks.com

HODOPHILE BOOKS

Don't miss out!

Visit the website below and you can sign up to receive emails whenever D.R. Ransdell publishes a new book. There's no charge and no obligation.

https://books2read.com/r/B-A-GBGI-WETTG

BOOKS 2 READ

Connecting independent readers to independent writers.